For Eileen with love   AM
Here's a book for Katie Rook   S J-P

VIKING
Published by the Penguin Group
Viking Penguin, a division of Penguin Books USA Inc.,
375 Hudson Street, New York, New York 10014, U.S.A.
Penguin Books Australia Ltd, Ringwood, Victoria, Australia
Penguin Books Canada Ltd, 2801 John Street, Markham, Ontario, Canada L3R 1B4
Penguin Books (N.Z.) Ltd, 182-190 Wairau Road, Auckland 10, New Zealand

First published in Great Britain by ABC 1990
First American edition published in 1990

10 9 8 7 6 5 4 3 2 1

Text © Angela McAllister 1990
Illustrations © Susie Jenkin-Pearce 1990

Library of Congress catalog number: 90-50074

ISBN 0-670-83376-2

Printed and bound in Hong Kong by Imago Services (HK) Ltd.

Nesta The Little Witch

Story by **Angela McAllister**

Illustrations by **Susie Jenkin-Pearce**

VIKING

All the little witches at The School for Spells worked hard at their lessons, but Nesta, the smallest witch, worked hardest of all.

Every evening, after school, she practiced spells and potions on all her family at home.

Sometimes her mother really didn't have the time to be turned into a giant toad, and sometimes her father didn't enjoy hanging upside-down like a bat, but they wanted Nesta to do well at school.

Her teachers, wicked Windbag Wartnose and mean Morag the Hag, were cruel and nasty and difficult to please. They enjoyed giving the little witches long, complicated, witchy things to learn.

There were potions to curl up people's toes, turn their fingers into candlesticks and their noses into corkscrews, and spells to make people sing "I'm a little teapot" non-stop for one week.

The little witches had to learn how to make things disappear with sparks and coloured smoke; how to cackle and screech loudly enough to make people's hair stand on end; how to talk to black cats and bats and how to fly on a broomstick.

It was no wonder that the little witches
always made mistakes.

"Is it 'lice and mice' or 'fleas and bees'?"
wondered mixed-up Min, as she tried to
brew up a thunderstorm.

But BAZAM! The sky
filled with rainbows
and a pot of gold
fell on her head.

"Is it 'zip, zap, zoom' or 'viz, vim, vroom'?" wondered mumbly Meg, as she tried to control her broomstick.

But WHOOOAAGHHH! The broomstick turned a double loop-the-loop, rolled upside-down and crashed into a chimney-pot.

"Is it 'eye of toad and…um…wing of bat, eagle's claw and serpent's…er… fang, lizard's…tail and beetle's breath,

and powdered hoof…no…horn of unicorn'?" wondered muddleheaded Mona, as she tried to turn her cat into an umbrella.

But WHIZZBANG! The cat turned into a monster with the eyes of a toad, the wings of a bat, the claws of an eagle, the fangs of a serpent, the tail of a lizard, the breath of a beetle and the horn of a unicorn!

The only one who never made
a mistake was Nesta, the little witch.

But Windbag Wartnose and Morag the Hag didn't like Nesta for being so clever. They thought she was a smartypants.
"Even her cauldron is always polished," they sneered. And so, being wicked witches, they did what wicked witches do best. They decided to trick Nesta into making a mistake.

The next day, when
the little witches were
given a spell to make
it rain cats and dogs,
Windbag Wartnose
and Morag the Hag
changed the words
on Nesta's spell.

One by one, Nesta put all the wrong ingredients into her cauldron: "Um...the toenails of a ladybird, that's easy...some poison ivy, plenty of that...a dozen fresh spiders' webs... whoops! With a couple of fresh spiders...and two pints of nettle juice...yuk!"

Wicked Windbag Wartnose and Morag the Hag cackled secretly in the shadows. They couldn't wait to see Nesta's face when her spell didn't turn out quite as she expected. "That'll teach her to be so clever, hee hee hee!"

They were so busy sniggering, they didn't see muddleheaded Mona's last mistake, which had also been hiding in the shadows and was now looking for lunch.

Just as Nesta gave her spell a final stir,
Mona's monster gave a loud BURP!
And that was all that was left of Windbag
Wartnose and Morag the Hag!
But the monster was still hungry. His boggle
eyes stared greedily at little Nesta, Mona,
Meg and Min.

The little witches shook with fear. Not even clever Nesta could remember a disappearing spell for monsters.

Suddenly, there was an explosion in Nesta's
cauldron and out of the sky fell, not cats
and dogs, but elephants and hippos.
And, just as the monster stretched out his
claws towards the little witches, four
elephants landed on top of him
with a SPLAT!

Nesta realised at once what Windbag Wartnose and Morag the Hag had done. Mona, Meg and Min were all very glad that, just this once, Nesta had surprised them all.

Together, the little witches tried to fix the spell but, by the time they had found the right words, there were elephants and hippos piling up everywhere.

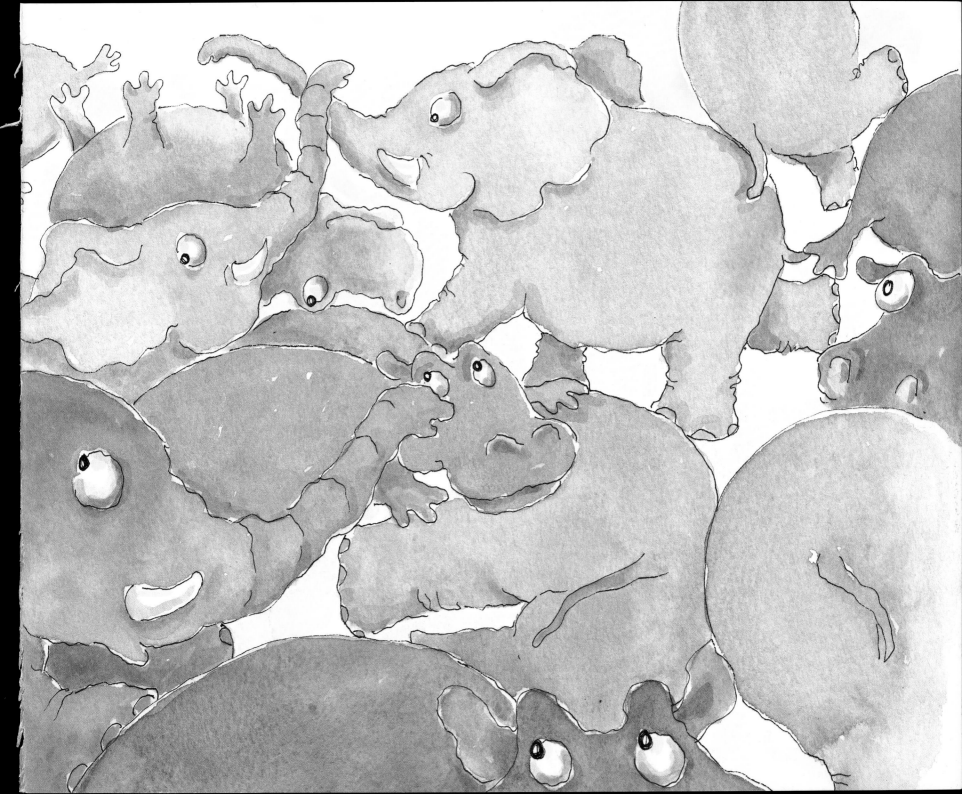

"What we need are some willing helpers!" said
Nesta. And, with a smelly puff of green smoke,
she brought back Windbag Wartnose and
Morag the Hag, looking all gobbled
and more horrible than before. But
Nesta the little witch
wasn't afraid.

"No more tricks today," she warned, as
she handed the two grumpy witches a
dustpan and brush. "Otherwise, I
just might make a real mistake,
a monster mistake—too big
for a little witch to fix!"